Funny Bone Readers™

Facing Your Fears

The Fable of The Bully Dragon

by Jeff Dinardo • illustrated by Livia Coloji

RED CHAIR PRESS

Please visit our website at **www.redchairpress.com**.
Find a free catalog of all our high-quality products for young readers.

Publisher's Cataloging-In-Publication Data
(Prepared by The Donohue Group, Inc.)

Dinardo, Jeffrey.
   The fable of the bully dragon : facing your fears / by Jeff Dinardo ; illustrated by
Livia Coloji. -- [First edition].

   pages : illustrations ; cm. -- (Funny bone readers. Dealing with bullies)

   Summary: Ming and her family harvest rice at the base of a tall mountain. They
could sell the extra rice at market on the other side of the mountain but the dragon on
the mountain steals the rice. Ming decides to try on her own to get past the dragon so
she packs up her ox and heads to the market. When the bully dragon tries to stop her,
Ming outwits the bully and makes it safely to market and back home with the money.
Includes glossary, as well as questions to self-check comprehension.
   Interest age level: 004-008.
   Edition statement supplied by publisher.
   Issued also as an ebook.
   ISBN: 978-1-63440-000-8 (library hardcover)
   ISBN: 978-1-63440-001-5 (paperback)

   1. Rice farmers--Juvenile fiction. 2. Bullying--Juvenile fiction. 3. Dragons--Juvenile
fiction. 4. Rice farmers--Fiction. 5. Bullying--Fiction. 6. Dragons--Fiction. I. Coloji,
Livia. II. Title.

PZ7.D6115 Fa 2015
[E]   2014958268

This series first published by:
Red Chair Press LLC   PO Box 333   South Egremont, MA 01258-0333

Printed in the United States of America

042015 1P WRZF15

Ming lives with her parents at the base of a tall mountain. They grow rice in the fields. But they are very poor.

Every Spring Ming's family harvests the rice. They have plenty for themselves. And there is a lot of extra rice!

"If we sold the rice at the
market we could earn money,"
said Ming's mother.

"But the dragon lives between us and the market," said her father. "He steals everything we bring."

"I am a big girl now," said Ming.
"I can take the rice to market."

"It is too dangerous," say her parents.
But Ming is determined.

Early the next day she sets out
with the rice tied to the ox.

Ming remembers tales her father told
her about dragons.
"I will not give him our rice!" she says
to herself. "I will be brave."

Ming slowly makes her way across the mountain. The path leads to a cave. There she sees the dragon.

"I smell rice," he snarls.
"Give it to me or I will eat you!"

Ming places the rice on the ground.
"I have met many dragons," Ming
boasts. "Many greater than you."
The bully dragon snarls.

"I met one dragon who could make himself as large as a temple," she says. The dragon laughs. "I can make myself twice as big." And he does.

"I have met a dragon who
could turn himself into a small
bail of hay." Ming said.

The dragon laughs. "I can make myself as tiny as a single blade of grass." And he does.

Ming quickly picks up the
grass and feeds it to the ox.

One bite and it is gone.

Ming repacks the bag of rice onto the ox and continues to the market. She sells all the extra rice.

Then Ming and the ox make the
long journey home.

"Ming, how did you get past the bully
dragon?" asks her proud father.

"I wasn't scared," explains Ming.
"A bullying, boastful dragon is no
match for a smart girl."

With no bully dragon to bother them, the family had much success at the market.

Big Questions: Do you think Ming was brave or foolish to face the bully dragon? How did Ming get past the dragon?

Big Words:

boastful: showing too much pride and self-confidence

determined: being willing to make a firm decision and not change it

snarls: speaks or makes noises in a mean way, as a threat.